Push the Dog

Allan Ahlberg

Colin McNaughton

WALKER BOOKS

LONDON

the girls

the boys

the dog

The boys push the dog

up the hill.

The girls pull the dog

down the hill.

The robbers put the dog

in a sack.

The police take the dog
out of the sack...

...and put the robbers in it!

The elephant gives the dog a ride.

The giant gives him
a bone.

And the ghosts give him a fright!

Mr Monster
takes the dog
for a walk.

Mrs Monster
bakes the dog
in a pie.

He eats his way out

. . . and goes home.

the basket

the dog

the end

Picture Dictionary

robber
sack
pie
policeman
moon
stars

hat
elephant
giant
ghost
kennel

bone